A Sicilian Family

CAROL CAICO

Fulton Books
Meadville, PA

Published by Fulton Books 2024

ISBN 979-8-88982-365-0 (paperback)
ISBN 979-8-88982-367-4 (hardcover)
ISBN 979-8-88982-366-7 (digital)

Printed in the United States of America

I sincerely thank Fulton Books and Ian Backer Literary Agent who was available to answer all my questions and called me that my book was going to be published. I thank Liz Bosley Publication Assistant and the Editors for all their help. You have helped every step of way.

I would like to dedicate this book to my deceased husband and know he would be so proud. I would like to thank my family for understanding the time it takes to write a book.

P R E F A C E

This book is about an Italian family who grew up in Palermo, Sicily. The young married couple had their four children there, and an occurrence with the daughter caused embarrassment, forcing them to leave their lives and move to America. There are many twists and turns during the lives of Maria and Mario and their children. There is great sadness as well as joyful times. This book is totally fictional, and I hope you enjoy following the lives of this family.

The Family

*Sometimes in life, there are many twists and
turns, and when life seems to be going well, there
are always dark changes around the corner.*

Maria was thirteen years old when she fell in love with Mario, who was fifteen years old. Maria had beautiful long thick black hair and brown eyes framed by long black eyelashes, was five feet four inches tall, and had a beautiful figure, which caught Mario's eye. Mario DiDomico had a great build for a teenager; a chiseled, handsome face; black hair; and brown eyes. Maria's parents, Francesca and Antonio Abbruzzo, had a good friend named Alessandro Mancuso. He visited often and was often invited to Sunday dinners with the family. Alessandro was single and had graying hair, heavy eyebrows, and a large stomach. He appreciated Maria's beauty and spoke to Francesca and Antonio requesting to date Maria with the intention of marrying her. Alessandro was fifty-two years old and older than Maria's father. The parents thought it would be a good match as Alessandro had great wealth from working at a bank and an inheritance from his deceased parents. Maria's sisters—Canelora, who was sixteen, and Centina, who was seventeen—still lived at home. Both of the sisters were plain-looking, and although both had boyfriends, neither of the boys were serious about the girls. They were jealous of Maria, as she was the beauty of the family. They wished Alessandro paid attention to them instead of Maria. Alessandro always directed his conversation to Maria and asked her one evening after dinner to take a walk. Maria refused. Her parents became angry with her and called her into her bedroom and closed the door. They both yelled at her for being so rude and told her she should marry Alessandro. She became hysterical crying and told her parents she loved Mario and not some fat old man. The parents became extremely angry, asking her, "What can Mario give you? He is young and *e stupido*!"

She continued crying and said, "I will marry Mario. Let one of my sisters marry the old man." Her parents told her she would not be permitted to see Mario, as she was now only fourteen and Mario was sixteen. They had no idea that they were seeing each other since she was thirteen and Mario was fifteen. They would see each other at school, and after school, they would sneak to spend time together. Mario was Maria's first love, and her heart would break each time they parted. Allesandro felt if Maria would not marry him and at age fifty two it was time he married. He started dating Centina. They married her a year later when she was eighteen and Alessandro was fifty-three. She was no way near as pretty as Maria, but Centina would make a good wife for Alessandro. They had a nice wedding, and her two sisters were bridesmaids. The parents knew that Maria would marry Mario. When Maria was nineteen and Mario was twenty-one and started his own business, her parents gave them a wedding. Maria looked so beautiful, and they were so happy together. Mario's parents, Alessia and Niero, loved Maria and was thrilled for them. They married on March 3, 1947. They knew that they wanted children soon after they purchased a large two-story stone house with large property and a huge basement in Palermo, Sicily, where they both grew up. Both Maria's parents and Mario's parents had their own one-story houses within walking distance to Maria and Mario's house. None of them had a car, as streets were narrow, and a passing car had to wait until it passed before a waiting car could proceed. Luckily all was in walking distance. Maria and Mario's first child was a beautiful 8.5-pound boy with a head of black hair and was born on December 10, 1947. They named him Giovani. Maria felt it was a rough vaginal delivery, and she had him at the local hospital and came home in three days. Maria was in considerable discomfort and was nervous taking care of the infant. Her mother, having three girls, told Maria she did not know how to take care of boys. Her mother-in-law helped, and soon Maria was an expert and breastfed Giovani. Her second son was born on September 19,1948, and although he was 7.5 pounds, it was a much easier delivery, and she came home from the hospital in two days. They named him Lorenzo, and he also had dark hair. Maria was now breastfeeding the two boys. She felt like she never stopped. She would clean the big house, be up with the babies at night, breastfeed either of the boys every two to three hours, and cook dinner for Mario, who worked all day. Both mothers would come over to help her. They had their third son on July 15, 1949. He was only seven pounds and two ounces, and again she was home from the hospital in two days. They named him Vincenzo, and he also had a head full of dark hair. All of the boys were beautiful. The toughest delivery was Giovani, as he was the biggest baby. She stopped breastfeeding Giovani, but she was still breastfeeding the other two boys. She and Mario thought they were finished having babies, when she became pregnant again. They were both extremely fertile, having children every nine months. She just assumed it would be another boy. On May 3, 1950, she had a beautiful girl. They were all thrilled, and they named her Ariana, which means "pure and holy." She was the most beautiful baby. Lorenzo was weaned, but Maria was still feeding Vincenzo and Ariana. People always stopped to stare at Ariana when she takes her out in her pram. Mario and Maria felt so fortunate to have four beautiful and healthy children. Both grandparents adored their grandchildren and helped whenever they could. Mario worked all the time to support them, and they wanted nothing.

They were a very religious Catholic family and went to Caledrala di Palermo every Sunday and then had their Sunday dinner together. Before the meal, they would enjoy olives grown by Mario, provolone, and mozzarella cheese with crusty homemade Italian bread. Each Sunday, Maria would make homemade meatballs, a large pot of homemade red sauce and sausage, and enough pasta for any guest who may come by. Sometimes, even during the week, they would eat together and have pasta with fresh vegetables from her garden. On Sundays, both grandmothers would make homemade cannoli, which

Sicily is known for. Occasionally, Maria's mother's grandmother, called Nona Clementina, would come for some Sunday dinner. She was ninety-seven but still mentally sharp, although suffering from aches and pains of old age. When she would come to dinner, she would talk very loud due to some loss of hearing. She said, "Ariana 'e aopprezzata per la sua bellezza per quando il bambino diventa teenager I problem aumentno" (Ariana is known for her beauty, but when the teenager years start, the problems will start). Ariana was hurt by this comment and worried about her future.

Usually, at their meals, everyone would talk at the same time, and some conversations would become heated, but no one gets angry, as forgiveness and love would always prevail. When Nona Clementina would come to Maria and Mario's house, she liked to dominate the conversation, and that Sunday, after insulting Ariana, she proceeded on telling the history of Sicily. It was somewhat interesting to the adults but boring for the children. They listened for some of it in respect to their great-grandmother. Maria told them they could go upstairs or go outside and play ball. Nona Clementina spoke of the history she lived through. She spoke of the many types of people who lived in Sicily, the Greeks, Muslims, and Turks. They eventually left when living became hard in Sicily. She spoke of the great depression as well as living through World War II. She gave graphic detail and said, "Thousands of Sicilians died, and many were maimed. When the allies targeted the Germans and their supplies, they dropped the bomb." The badly damaged cities included Messina, Catania, and Augusta on the east coast and Palermo and Trapani in the west. Things that were bought pre-war were gone after the war, and nothing could be bought not even matches. People were destitute, hungry, defenseless, and terrified. The Sicilians having a hot meal were just a memory. The Americans and British were provisional government while driving the Germans out. Sicily had been the Mafia stronghold. The Fascists drove them out in 1925, but when the Fascists left, the mafioso were back strong again. There was much strife in Sicily, and in 1946, Sicily went from a kingdom to a republic to an autonomous region. It would take two years for Italy's new constitution to enact it. In 1948, there was an election, and

Sicily's threat of separatism allowed Sicily its own local government, which had responsibility for the island's agriculture, fishing industry, and commerce, public works, museums, libraries, tourism, and primary instruction. In the years 1848–1948, probably more than any previous century, Sicily experienced momentous episodes.

Two weeks after Nona Clementina shared the history of her life, she died in her sleep. She was just 98. Her husband died when she was forty-two from a flu epidemic. They all attended the wake, the funeral mass, and burial. It was the first time the children had seen a dead person, and after the funeral, the children became anxious for fear that their grandparents and parents would die. They were assured that Nona Clementina was very old when she died. The four children were growing up so fast. Ariana was eight, and the boys were nine, ten, and eleven. Mario and Maria took precaution against pregnancy, as four children was enough, especially nine months apart. They had all the teenage years ahead of them, and the thought of what Nona Clementina warned about Ariana's beauty and the teenage years would be a problem.

The children all did well in school and were learning English as a second language. They would hear them practicing words with each other. They were all active in sports, and Maria including the grandparents went to every game. Mario tried, but with his business, sometimes, he would not make it to the games. Ariana and the boys had many friends, and Ariana complained that all the boys in class stare at her. She was very beautiful all the time. She had long thick brown hair with beautiful blond highlights from the sun and greenish-blue eyes. Mario found out that his great-grandmother had light eyes. Mario works hard to provide for his family, but Maria and the kids wanted nothing, as they all had what they needed. Maria was a housewife and kept her home immaculate and made wonderful meals with fresh vegetables from her garden for her family. She was a wonderful mother. They lived in a large two-story stone house. Giovani as the oldest had his own room, Lorenzo and Vincenzo shared a large room, and Ariana had her own completely pink room. They lived in a beautiful part of Palermo, right by the Mediterranean sea and the beach. The children spent time at the beach with each other and their friends. "C e un cielo azzurro" (The sky is azure).

The temperature range in Sicily in the winter is 54 and rarely goes below, while in the spring and summer, it is 87 and rarely goes above. The breeze from the sea, which was wonderful, kept them comfortable in the warm months. They all grew up in Palermo. Maria's sister Centina was still married to Alessandro and had two children, Bruno, sixteen, and Gabriella, fifteen. They did not stay in Palermo but moved to Naples. Her sister Canelora was set up by a friend and fell in love and married for love. She and her husband, Claudio Greco, had two boys, Angelo, eleven, and Rocco, twelve, and lived in Cantania, which was about a three-and-a-half-hour drive. Mario's brother Carman and his wife, Bianca, only had one daughter, Gina, ten. There was trouble with Gina's birth, and Bianca could never have more children. They moved to Rome, where Carman had a job. Mario's sister Chiara and her husband, Matteo, had two children, a boy named after his father, Matteo Jr., thirteen, and a girl Lucia, twelve, and lived also live in Cantania. They all would try to get together for Christmas and Easter and come to the beach in the summer. Maria's sister Centina sometimes would come alone with the children because she did not want Alessandro to still have regrets about Maria, who was still very pretty. It still bothered Centina, although she had a good marriage; when she would see Maria, she would feel that she was Alessandro's second choice.

Mario

Mario DiDomico had a very large piece of property beyond Maria's vegetable garden. Mario grew olives and had five large arbors filled with grapes and also had many grape trees. He had a large basement with all his equipment for his lucrative business. He also employed many to harvest the grapes and the olives when ripe. Most were men, but one was a twenty-four-year-old female, Lina Vitali, who worked as hard as the men. Originally, when Mario started his business when he and Maria were married, he pressed the grapes himself and put the extracted juice into glass bottles with a device on top of the bottles to keep air out. At the time, he only used Nero q' Avolo grapes. When the juice fermented, he put the wine in dark bottles and corked the bottles and sold the wine to many stores all over Sicily under the name DiDomico Wine. He charged $35 a bottle, as the process to make the red wine was arduous. He also had many Castelvetrano olive trees. He invested money from his wine sales to buy the machinery to press the olive juice from the olives, mix them with water, separate the clean olive extract through a series of racks, and then pour the virgin olive oil into bottles via a conveyor belt. The name on the label was DiDomico Family Virgin Olive Oil. He was optimistic that his sons would join the business. To retrieve the olives from the trees, he paid helpers to rake to the olives, which shakes the olives from the trees when the olives are ripe. The workers would then transport the olives to the machine area. Virgin olive oil was used by all Italians, and Mario would travel all over Italy, selling his olive oil at $45 a bottle. Sales were great, allowing him to plant other grapes and purchase machinery and large steel vats to make different types of wines under his name. He enjoyed making money and providing well for his family. He tried to finish work in time to eat with his family, unless he was traveling promoting his products. It seemed his children were getting older, and with him working so much, he realized they were all getting older.

Ariana was fourteen, and although her brothers watched out for her, she fell in love with Antonio La Rosa. She had to sneak to see him as her brothers tried to keep her from doing what she wanted. Maria understood and felt it was only "puppy love," even though Maria loved Mario at that age. Mario was so busy with the business, keeping the books, paying all the workers, and being the boss, who made sure their jobs were to his satisfaction. Mario started to export his olive oil to the USA as well. The wine production grew as he started growing novella cataratta and nerello mascalese, frescolio novella grapes, which allowed him to make Cabernet Sauvignon, Chianti, a light white wine and an affordable red table wine. He became known for his excellent wines and his delicious light virgin olive oil. He started a huge export business to the USA and got orders from all over Italy, and all stores carried his olive oil as well as all his wines. His name was well known, and his empire began to grow. He even started exporting to England. He became very smug with his success and did not ask how Maria's day was or the kids but just spoke of all he did and would say, "That is why you have such beautiful clothes and jewelry due to me." He started expecting the boys to help him and informed them "they would inherit the business one day and must learn all there is to know about it." The only one really interested in the business was Giovani. Lorenzo and Vincenzo wanted to go to a university and become professionals with degrees.

Mario got a call in his office and felt like he was punched in the gut after finding out that his father died. His mother called him crying on the phone and told him his father died of lung cancer.

Mario started screaming. "Why didn't you tell me!"

She replied, "You are so busy, you really do not know what is going on outside of your work."

Mario replied, "I thought he had a cold with a cough." Mario broke down and sobbed. It was finally a humbling time for him.

The children were very depressed losing one of their grandparents. The dynamics of the family was greatly altered. He was loved by many, and many people attended his wake, the funeral mass, and burial in a beautiful spot under a tree. Everyone in the family cried and felt his loss immensely.

Mario grieved his father for a long time and spent more time with his family. Two weeks later, he had a business to run and returned to work, but to him, Sunday dinners would make his dad's death more apparent. They left his chair at the table empty for a long time. Mario was still angry with his mother for not informing him of his father's cancer and felt he would have spent more time with him and did not get to say goodbye to him. He became despondent and got angry easily even to his employees, which was unlike him. He said to Maria, "I am waiting for the next shoe to drop." He anticipated troubles were around the corner.

Ariana

Ariana's brother seemed to always be watching her as she was fifteen and a half and more beautiful all the time. Her hair was very long, down to her lower back, with beautiful highlights. She felt she could not spread her wings due to their constant scrutiny. She was happy when Giovani, at nineteen and a half, had a girlfriend and Lorenzo and Vincenzo were also interested in girls. Ariana started to sneak out to see Roberto, whom she professed her love to.

Roberto adored her. He was seventeen and planned on attending college and becoming an architect. He told Ariana he planned to marry her. He gave her a very small promise ring. They made out every chance they could but only kissed although very passionately. Eventually, teenage hormones started raging, and Roberto began opening Ariana's blouse and feeling her breasts. She responded with moans of pleasure. This continued for months until he started to remove her shorts and began putting his fingers around a sensitive area she did not even knew existed. She writhed with pleasure.

Roberto's parents work many hours, as they owned a trattoria called LaRosa's. Antonio knew when his parents left for work and when they would come home. He spent as much alone time with Ariana as possible. She felt a hardness when he was kissing her or touching her. Ariana wondered what he had in his pants and felt it and thought it was a cigarette lighter or a big rock that he saved. Ariana noticed he was breathing heavily when she wondered what was in his pants. She asked him what was in his pants. He proceeded to unzip his pants to show her, and she became shocked at the site of the hard thing with the purple top. Roberto already had Ariana's pants off and touched her as she liked and also felt her breasts. He explained to her, "What you called a thing is a penis and go inside of you."

Her hormones were numbing her brain. She loved him and had a promise ring that he would marry her, so she told him, "Okay, let's try it." She screamed after he put it in her. She cried and saw blood on "the thing you called a penis."

He assured her. "The next time will not hurt but will feel good." He began sucking her breasts, and Ariana felt so good, she forgot the pain. Roberto told her he loved, and she told him she loved him and left to go home.

Ariana came home and told her mother she was studying at Nicholetta's house. Her mother said, "That is great, to keep your marks up studying with friends."

Sicilians regard the family as the most important. The mother is at the center of all the familial relationships. She is the glue that holds the family together: "Casa mia, matri mia!" (My home, my mother!) While Sicilian society is patriarchal, the father provides for his family.

Maria would sacrifice anything for her children. She became concerned when a couple of months passed and Ariana did not ask her mother to purchase sanitary pads for her period. She asked Maria when her last period was, and Maria could not remember. Maria became worried and felt there could be a medical problem, so she brought her to Dr. Caruso. He checked Ariana and checked her urine and drew some blood. He called them both into the office and said, "The urine looks like she is pregnant. We will confirm with the bloodwork."

Maria began tearfully yelling, "No, no, no!" She grabbed her arm, and they left the office. When they left the doctor's office, she asked Ariana, "How can this be?"

She told her mother she was with Roberto and she loves him. She was naive too. How could she have gotten pregnant when she said she had her period 2 weeks before? Ariana said to Maria they only did it once.

Maria said, "This is the time of the month you can get pregnant, but the real issue is why did this happen? How many times were you alone with him to get to this point?"

Ariana told her mother they only did it once.

"You will not see him again, and I will talk to his parents, and we will decide what to do. You are not having a baby at sixteen."

Maria never had sex with Mario before marriage, although they were very fertile, and she thought that if Ariana only had sex with Roberto once, then she must be very fertile also. Maria recalled Nona Clementina's words about Ariana's beauty and problems in the teenage years. Maria never expected it would be this. Maria called Dr. Caruso, and the blood confirmed she was two months pregnant. Although terminations were not legal, she asked the doctor if he knew of anyone reputable to go to.

He said, "As a friend, I know of a Doctor Ricci in Pompeii, but do not say I gave you his name please."

Maria was in her bedroom when Mario came home for dinner. She had cooked dinner earlier and just heated the vegetables and made pasta. Mario went to the bedroom to find out what was happening with her. Maria told Mario what happened, and he was shocked. His first instinct was to go and take it out on Roberto, but Maria said they both were at fault and Ariana claimed she loves him. Maria was tearful and said, "We are so religious, but I am going to fly with her to Pompeii to I le medico Ricci and schedule an abortion." Maria added, "Mi senta sono ammaltata" (I feel sick). Maria asked Mario, "Can you make reservations for a flight as soon as possible from Palermo International (Falcone Borsellino) to Pompeii and a hotel for two days and a return flight. I will go to confession the Saturday when I return."

Maria called Roberto's family and informed them what happened. They were very upset and said they both own a Trattoria and are there a lot of the time and felt so guilty because they never expected their son to be alone with Ariana and have intercourse in their home. They offered to do anything to help. Maria thanked them and informed them that Ariana could no longer see Roberto.

Maria and Ariana left three days later. When they arrived in Pompeii, they took a taxi to Dr. Ricci's office. Maria begged him to perform the procedure that day. He agreed but told them to wait. They waited two hours, and Ariana started to cry, as she was religious too and knew that the church did not believe in abortion. She was also nervous about the procedure. When she was called in, the doctor performed a sonogram to make sure she was only two months pregnant. He gave her a local and did not want to give her anesthesia.

Ariana heard the scraping of her uterus and felt a little pain and then heard a machine removing "her baby." They both left after she spent one hour in the recovery room to make sure all was okay. The doctor gave her a prescription for three days of antibiotics. Maria and Ariana went to the hotel. After, she went to the pharmacy for the prescription of antibiotics and some pads for her bleeding after the pregnancy termination.

Ariana rested, and Maria took wine from the bar in the hotel room, as she felt shaky after the entire ordeal. They returned home in two days. Her brothers were upset, and again, the family dynamics were changed. Maria's parents were told the truth, and they reminded them that Ariana's name meant "holy and pure."

The entire family was upset, and change loomed in the future. Mario and Maria were very upset with their one daughter. Ariana was worried that her parents would possibly move to save face. Ariana sneakily called Roberto and told him that she still loved him and hope they would see each other again someday when they can finally be together.

C H A P T E R 4

Giovani

Giovani was now twenty years old and was the only son interested in his father's business. He had helped him since he was about fourteen. He was very familiar about keeping the proceeds from both the various wines and olive oil. He learned how to run the machines and planned on taking over the business someday.

One day, he went home for lunch, and his mother had cheese, Italian bread, and tomatoes from the garden. Mario was busy at work, and he was now despondent over his one daughter's pregnancy and abortion. Maria had been drinking more wine for the guilt in taking part of Ariana's abortion. Even though Maria went to confession, she still was consumed with guilt.

Mario's one female worker, Lina Vitali, was now almost twenty-seven and had a very sexy figure with big breasts. Mario became attracted to her, and she idolized her boss for giving her the job. That day, he brought her past the machine and proceeded to kiss her. Things became very heated. Lina began breathing very fast and unbuttoned her blouse, and Mario proceeded touching her large breasts.

Giovani returned from lunch and looked for his father but did not call him, as Giovani figured he was by the machines. He walked around looking for him and came upon his father kissing and touching Lina Vitali's breasts. He felt like his heart would stop when he saw them. Mario sensed someone was there, and when he saw Giovani, he wanted to run and cry. Lina closed her blouse and went back to work.

Mario had to talk to Giovani and beg him to tell no one, especially his mother. Mario said, "It would never happen again, and I'm so sorry it happened." He also said he loved Maria, who was now almost forty, while he was forty-two. He tried to explain further. "The last time that this happened was with Ariana's problem and his father's death. I was feeling sad, and it just happened. Please forgive me." Mario was embarrassed and feeling very guilty.

Appearances in a Sicilian family is very important. The sense of pride that attaches to the individual comes into play for his family. The loss of face of one member cannot fail to have some effect on the pride of the family as a unit. "Cui perdi la bona fama perdi tuttu" (He who loses his reputation loses everything).

Ariana's pregnancy and his father's indiscretion affected Giovani greatly. His mother was still beautiful, and he had grown up believing they would never stray from one another. He could never hurt his mother by ever telling her what he witnessed with his father.

With the recent situation that happened in the family, Mario decided to move Maria and Ariana to the USA. The mafioso in Sicily charged all of businesses in stores all over Sicily to pay them a fee, and if they refused, there were consequences.

Mario's business was in the basement of his house, and they never bothered his family. Giovani knew the business as well as Mario, so he fired Lina Vitali and hired another man. The workers were all dependable, and with his father moving to the USA, in the near future, he would run the daily operations and continue to export all to Italy and the USA, and Mario would pick all the imports at the New York docks.

Mario would travel to Sicily every two months to assess the harvest of grapes and the olive crop. Mario would continue to make considerable money and pay Giovani handsomely. Mario kept the house in Sicily where Giovani lived.

Lorenzo and Vincenzo both went to the Libre Universita Del Sicilian Central Kore, and when they had any weeks off the university, they would return to the house. Lorenzo and Vincenzo both wanted to become architects and considered moving to the USA to open a firm. In the Universita, they have perfected their English.

They both started college together, were in several classes together, and would graduate together.

Mario was supporting them while they were in the Universita but wished they cared about the business, but they were never interested, as Giovani only had interest. Mario, Maria, and Ariana flew to the USA and went to Bensonhurst, where cousins had come to America years before on a ship. They lived on the top floor of an apartment, above their cousin. It was a large-enough apartment, and there were a lot of Italian grocery stores and fruit markets, so Maria cooked the way she was used to. Ariana was enrolled in an all-girls Catholic high school within walking distance. Everyone talked Italian, so they felt right at home. People sat on the stoop at night and met all the neighbors.

Giovani met the love of his life when he was shopping for food. She was also shopping, and their carts banged into each other going down one of the isles. He called his family in America and said, "We started talking, and it was like love at first sight. She is beautiful, and her name is Bella Trapani. I have been dating her for three months now and know I will marry her. I hope you will all come home for our wedding when it happens. I will certainly give you enough notice. I know eventually Grandma and Grandpa will plan on moving to America, but I hope everyone will come to my wedding. "Holidays will never be the same with aunts, uncles, and cousins coming. I miss you, Mom and Ariana. Dad, I see you every two months. What about Sunday dinners? Maybe both grandmothers could cook on Sundays. I guess life has changed, and I don't know if it is for the better. I am busy with the business and hope you are receiving all the wines and olive oil I exported to the New York docks."

He spoke to his mother, "I am lonely at night, as there is always noise and I am alone in the house. Maybe I'll get a dog to keep me company."

His mother thought it was a great idea. She told him, "I can't wait to meet Bella. I will come with Dad on his next visit. I miss you and Lorenzo and Vincenzo."

C H A P T E R   5

Living in America

Maria and Mario were sick of apartment living and missed living by the water. They waited until Ariana graduated from high school on June 26, 1968, at eighteen. They had a party for her, and the neighbors, cousins, and some of Ariana's classmates came to celebrate her graduation. Mario purchased a car and practiced driving because in Palermo, they walked as everything was close. Mario's father taught him to drive when he was young, but he felt he needed to brush up. When he finally felt confident, he drove out to Long Island in search of a house near water. They found a sprawling home on the water in a town called Massapequa in a section called Harbor Green.

There was a huge driveway for the car, a large garage, and a large basement. The backyard was large, and the property measured 150 feet by 200 feet. The houses were not close to each other, yet the community appeared to be a lovely community and was sure to have good neighbors.

They decided they wanted to become citizens of America. Ariana helped them learn English while attending an English class, and although they found the English language difficult to learn, they persevered. Mario and Maria wanted to fit into the community and had to learn English and study to be ready to become citizens. It took a year before they appeared before the judge who asked them many questions they were prepared for. They met all the requirements and were sworn in as citizens of the USA on July 26, 1970.

The house was expensive, and taxes were very high. The house was $67,000, which at the time was very high, and taxes were $22,000

17

per year. Mario's business was doing extremely well, and he drove to Foodtown and Waldbaum, which were chain supermarkets, and they all carried his olive oil, which sold out very fast. The wines were sold to many liquor stores for even higher prices than the prices in Sicily. He also sold to many local Italian markets. Giovani was running the business in Palermo, and Mario went to Palermo every two months to check on the grapes and olives and see how Giovani was doing. He was still going to the docks to pick up all the exports of wines and olive oil exported from Giovani.

Maria went to Palermo on Mario's next trip to meet Bella and saw her sons, whom she missed terribly. They stayed in the Palermo house, and after meeting beautiful Bella, she invited her parents to dinner to meet them. They were lovely people. Bella was an only child but loved being with Mario and Maria's large family.

Vincenzo and Lorenzo

Vincenzo and Lorenzo finished the university together. The program to become architects took five years. Lorenzo was now twenty-three, and Vincenzo was twenty-two. Their plan was to join their parents in America and start an architectural firm together. They wanted to design big buildings and large expensive homes. They planned to live with their parents until they start their business. All three boys were very handsome and had angular features with slim waists and broad shoulders. One could tell they were brothers.

Vincenzo and Lorenzo dated during their years at the university, as many girls were attracted to their good looks, but neither of them became serious with any girls, as their plan was mapped out.

Vincenzo and Lorenzo went home to Palermo and stayed with Giovani who was now twenty-four. While Giovani was busy working, Bella went to school and became an RN, and she worked in a hospital. Bella and Giovani set the wedding date for Saturday, June 19, 1971. They both planned a beautiful venue for the wedding, and Bella bought a magnificent wedding gown. Although Bella and Giovani could afford to pay for the wedding, Bella's parents and Mario insisted on paying for the wedding. The ceremony was in the church followed by a great reception. Maria's parents and sisters and their husbands came, and Mario's sister and her children and his brother and both spouses came as well as many friends of Bella and Giovani. The band was great, and everyone danced. It was so wonderful seeing the whole family.

Maria stayed in the Palermo house and became nostalgic as she raised her children there, but they were all adults now. She spent time looking at the clear blue color of the Mediterranean.

Bella and Giovani left for their honeymoon to London and England. Maria and Ariana stayed to take care of Giovani's black Labrador, Cosmo. He was very sweet, and they took him for walks. Ariana still loved Roberto, and on one of the walks, she saw Roberto and ran up to him and hugged him as tears streamed down her cheeks. Ariana was old enough to make her own decisions and spent the rest of her time with Roberto. They still loved each other and planned to get married.

When Bella and Giovani returned from their honeymoon and it was time for Ariana to go back to America, she begged Roberto to come with her. Roberto wanted to stay in Palermo for a time, as in their time apart, he attended a university and became an accountant and had a job and wanted to get as much experience as possible. Ariana tried to convince him he would make more money in New York and there was a need for accountants. He told her he would get a visa after he worked some more. He told her if all plans to come to America, he would become a citizen and marry her. Roberto had one brother, Marco, whom he did not get along with, and he said, "I will not miss him, and I rarely saw my parents as they were always at their Italian Trattoria."

When they were leaving for the airport to return to New York, she passionately kissed Roberto and cried and held onto him to the last minute.

Back to America

They all landed in America on June 29. Lorenzo and Vincenzo were amazed seeing New York from the air. They had never seen such large buildings. They landed at Kennedy Airport, which was the biggest airport they had ever seen. There was a car waiting for them to take them home to Massapequa.

Lorenzo and Vincenzo loved the big house on the water but was disappointed of the brownish water when they were used to the clear blue of the Mediterranean. They went outside to look at the property and found their father in a huge garden of tomatoes and asked him what he was doing with all the tomatoes. He informed them that he stated another business boiling off the skins adding basil and canning the plum tomatoes. He would export some to Giovani to send to Italian markets and will send to many local Italian markets in the Massapequa area. Some of the markets were Uncle Giuseppi, Ivarone, and Salpino and some as far as Babylon. Since the climate can only grow tomatoes in the summer, if it is a success, like most of his businesses are, he may build a hothouse to grow them all year. He informed the boys that he now owned trucks with two drivers that went to docks to pick up wines and olive oil and bring them to all markets that carry them. They would also bring the cans of tomatoes to the Italian Markets. Mario said, "I am getting older and worked hard all my life. I love to garden and enjoy growing the tomatoes."

While Ariana waited for Roberto to come to New York, she decided to go to Adelphi University to study accounting.

Mario told his sons, "You should start your architectural firm, and I will give you money to get started." Mario drove the boys around the island to find a good spot for the firm. They found a great spot in Garden City with two desks. Garden City had many businesses. Mario's lawyer helped them become citizens and helped them get insurance coverage on the business. Lorenzo and Vincenzo bought all the supplies they needed: blueprints, a blackboard to draw on, and small building material to build to show clients what the design would look like. They had a sign built for the top of the building, which said, "Brothers Architectural Firm Specializing in Large Buildings and Large Home Design."

The phone number was also listed, and when they were not in the office, the number was forwarded so that they would not miss a potential client. They stayed at their parents' house until the business became a success. Maria was thrilled to have three of her children home and cooked every night and a big meal on Sundays.

Lorenzo and Vincenzo started their firm eight months after they came to New York. Six months after they began their firm, it was successful and had clients waiting to be seen. They decided it was time to move out and found a large apartment in Garden City close to their office. They promised their mother they would come on Sundays for dinner. The boys worked hard.

While Ariana was in college, if weather was bad, she would stay at her brothers' apartment. Ariana continued with her studies and was in her last semester. She was now twenty-three years old. Lorenzo and Vincenzo worked at their firm over three years now. After devoting so much time to building their firm, they decided to go to a club one night. It was 1977. They met two girls who were attending a bachelorette party. The two pairs became interested with each other. Vincenzo liked Cecilia Greco, who majored in dance in college and successfully owned her own dance studio. Lorenzo liked Gianna Marino, a nurse practitioner in a private internal medicine office. They went out for coffee that night and talked like old friends. They started dating separately, and each took the girls to nice places, eventually falling in love.

Maria's Parents

Maria's parents, Francesca and Antonio Abbruzzo, flew to New York to live with her. Mario paid for their flight. It was the first time they had ever been on an airplane. They were both apprehensive to fly, but after take-off, they relaxed and enjoyed the flight. They loved seeing the big buildings while descending into Kennedy Airport. Mario and Maria picked them up and were so happy to see them. They were going to stay with Maria and Mario. Her parents loved the big house and all the property, but just like Vincenzo and Lorenzo, they were disappointed at the color of the water, as they had lived in Palermo all their lives and thought all water was the clear blue of the Mediterranean.

Francesca was now seventy-six, and Antonio was seventy-eight, but they had a lot of energy and always stayed busy. Francesca planned on cooking a lot of meals and helped around the house. Antonio loved the tomato garden and helped Mario with the canning. Mario did build the hothouse as the business was successful. The house was big enough, and with the boys gone, her parents had their own wing with their own bathroom.

They were so proud of Ariana and were excited to go to her graduation. They came on May 2, 1972, and Ariana graduated on May 20. She was allowed six tickets for her graduation, so her grandparents, parents, and brothers attended. All clapped when her name was announced, and most forgot the difficult time when she was a teenager and was pregnant. They all went out to an Italian restaurant after graduation and had antipasto, and they carried Mario's wine and ordered a bottle of the expensive red wine and ordered an entree of their choice. They enjoyed the food, and all spoke Italian because Maria's parents had not learned English. They planned to help them learn English, which took almost a year for them to start to speak English They all stayed religious and went to mass every Sunday together.

When Ariana told her grandparents that Roberto and she were in love and he would be coming to New York to marry her, her grandparents were shocked, as they remembered when Ariana got pregnant by Roberto at a young age, and could not understand that Maria would support the marriage. Maria explained to her mother that they loved one another for a long time and wrote to each other and spoke on the phone often. She also told her that both became an accountant, with Ariana studying to become a CPA.

Ariana found out yesterday that Roberto was coming. She started crying with happiness and asked Maria if they could they shop for a wedding gown. Ariana drove her car to pick Roberto up at Kennedy Airport. When they saw each other, they ran toward each other and kissed and did not want to stop. They held hands and went to the car and kissed again. They were both so happy, and before they got in the car, Roberto got down on one knee and took out the most beautiful diamond ring and asked her to marry him. She could not wait for the wedding. Roberto had been saving for the diamond ring while working as an accountant in Palermo. When they got back to the house, Ariana showed everyone the large diamond engagement ring. It was round, 2 1/2 K, with diamonds on both sides. The family congratulated them, and since Roberto wanted to become a citizen, Mario's lawyer started the process.

Ariana and Roberto wanted to start an accounting firm together after the wedding. Maria and her mother saw an exquisite wedding gown in a magazine and went to an exclusive wedding shop and found the gown. She tried it on, and it was decided that that was the one. She looked so lovely. She remained so beautiful with her very long hair with blondish highlights and her greenish eyes and long lashes.

Roberto was also very handsome, and they made a perfect couple. They set the date for Saturday, June 17, 1974. Ariana was now twenty-five, and Roberto was twenty-seven. Mario paid for an elaborate wedding for his only daughter. They were married in church, and the reception was held in Great Neck at Leonard Palazzo with Italian cuisine and beautiful landscape for great pictures of the bride and groom. They also had a bridal suite. They had limousines for the wedding party. Her brothers were in the wedding party along with two good friends. From the church to the reception, the band was terrific, and many friends and cousins from Bensonhurst came. Ariana had many friends, and they came to the wedding.

Roberto's parents closed their trattoria for their son and Ariana's wedding. They had a wonderful time at the wedding and stayed overnight at a hotel at the airport and left for home the next day as they had to open their trattoria.

Ariana and Roberto went on a honeymoon to Bermuda for seven days. When they returned from their honeymoon, their true love was obvious. Ariana went around in her car with Roberto looking for a place to start their accounting business. They found an ideal place in North Massapequa on Jerusalem Avenue. Since Mario helped his sons start their firm, he also helped his daughter and son-in-law start their accounting office. They purchased adding machines and computers. They also found a large apartment on the second floor of a lovely house in Second Street. The family who owned the house were an Italian couple and lived on the ground floor with their seven-month-old baby boy. They were happy Ariana and Roberto were also Italian.

The accounting office was called LaRosa's Accounting, and the sign on the top of the store was "We Manage All of Your Accounting Needs." The name of the practice was Roberto's last name LaRosa and Ariana's name now that they were married. They enjoyed working together and going home together. They loved being together, and Ariana became pregnant eight months after they were married. They were both very happy. Ariana felt great, and they continued to work together until she was ready to deliver.

Her parents and brothers were so excited for them. This would be the first grandchild for Maria and Mario. They had just found out that Bella was pregnant. Giovani was so happy she was five months pregnant. Maria and Mario went to Palermo when Bella was due. They had a beautiful girl and named her Rosemarie on September 4, 1986.

They were also excited with their second grandchild. Bella and Giovani were married June 19, 1971. Ariana and Roberto worked hard at their accounting firm, and it became very successful. Ariana became pregnant one year after the wedding and delivered an eight-pound baby boy on March 1976. He was christened Roberto Jr., but they would call him Robbie until he goes to school. The baby was big for Ariana, and she had a large episiotomy and was sore for two weeks. Roberto adored his son and his beautiful wife, Ariana. They were happy and looked forward to having more kids and a long and happy life together. They loved working together and going home together. Maria watched the baby when they were at the office. They often took their baby to the office and had a playpen there.

The practice was successful and now two years, and Robbie was a year old. Roberto began having headaches and dizziness. Ariana said, "You probably have a viral infection or the flu. Go and see the doctor. He may prescribe something for it."

Calamity

Roberto saw the doctor on October 1974. He ran a series of tests including blood work, a CT scan, and an MRI. Ariana was concerned and told the doctor, "Roberto probably has a viral infection or the flu, which was around. Roberto made light of it and tried to tell me it was nothing."

The doctor called them in after all the tests were in and wanted them to come in together. Ariana told Roberto, "I am sure he just wants to make more money on another visit to tell us all the tests were normal." The doctor asked them to sit. He came in with a chart and had all the tests before him. He put one of them on a large screen and used a pointer and said, "This is a tumor in your head, Roberto, and this is what is causing your headaches and dizziness. I want you to see Dr. Gerstein, an oncologist in Great Neck. The number is 516-379-2000."

Ariana broke down sobbing, and Roberto tried to comfort her. She was shaking so badly, she could not drive. Roberto drove the short distance to their apartment. Ariana called her parents who were watching the baby when they went to the doctor's office. She was still crying when she spoke to her mother. Maria took the baby as she also had a car seat and went to their apartment. Ariana told her mother while in tears what the doctor told them. Roberto kept trying to calm her down and assured her he would be treated and be fine. They both hugged their son. Ariana had been breastfeeding and pumped so her mother had breast milk to give the infant. When Ariana held her son and started breastfeeding, she calmed down a little. She had been so joyful and contented looking forward to a long and wonderful life with Roberto and having more children and working together in their accounting office.

They made an appointment on a Friday morning with the oncologist, and she pumped her breast again so that her mother could keep the baby when they visited the office. Her father decided to drive them, and he went next door to get a cup of coffee and would wait in the car for them. Dr. Gerstein was kind and reviewed all the tests and told them the tumor was cancer and in a spot that it could not be operated on. It was located at the base of his brain. The doctor informed him he would set Roberto up for chemotherapy followed by radiation to try to shrink the tumor to alleviate symptoms and extend his life.

Roberto asked, "If I do all of the treatment, will I live a long time?"

Dr. Gerstein said, "I want to be honest. If the tumor shrinks with the treatment and if the tumor comes back, we could try treatment again."

He was to start chemo at the cancer center across the street from Dr. Gerstein's office on Monday. He was scheduled for a weekly chemotherapy, and the time would be set for 10:00 a.m., which would take two hours to finish. The doctor did inform him he would lose his hair. Ariana tried to be brave, but she realized the severity of the situation and that at his young age, he would lose his beautiful black hair and suffer the side effects of three to four months of chemo followed by radiation.

She went home, got on her knees, and prayed that it would shrink and disappear and never come back. Ariana had thoughts that getting pregnant at a young age and having abortion was why this was happening.

Roberto had to call his parents to let them know but told them there was no need to come as he was being treated. However, his parents wanted to fly in to see him and their grandson. They only stayed for three days and had to return to Palermo to their *ristoratore*.

Ariana and Maria went to church every day and prayed to Jesus to cure Roberto and give them strength. They brought the baby in a stroller with them to church. Monday came too soon, and Ariana went with Roberto for his chemo. After the second chemo, his hair started falling out in clumps, and Mario helped him shave his head. He started wearing a baseball cap backward so he looked younger. The day after chemo, he vomited and felt sick but passed by the next day. He had to wear a patch to prevent his white count from going down. After the second month of chemo, Roberto developed sores in his mouth and was prescribed a medication for rinsing. Ariana's heart was broken seeing him suffer. "All this time, I had waited for my true love to come here, and I cannot stand to see him suffer," Ariana said.

Before he started chemo, the doctor suggested he have his sperm saved, which they may use for insemination if they wanted more children. He continued to try to be strong for Ariana and their son.

Every night, when Roberto would be asleep, Ariana would sit in the living room and cry. During the week, she would go to their accounting office and see clients to keep the practice to pay bills. During tax season, she would be busy all day until 7:00 p.m. On Mondays, she would not go in the office, as she would accompany Roberto for chemo.

After three-and-a-half months of chemo, tests were repeated. The tests showed the tumor shrunk a lot. Chemo was continued another month, and the radiation was scheduled every day. Roberto had no more headaches or dizziness. He just had chemo side effects. Radiation was next and was to be done every day. When Ariana was busy in the office, her father took Roberto for radiation. It lasted for two months, and Roberto had red burns on his head and became very fatigued.

Ariana continued to work to help pay the bills, and although they took health insurance when they had the baby, it did not pay all the costs of Roberto's treatments. Maria watched the baby, and both Maria and Mario and her brothers were heartbroken for what Ariana and Roberto were going through. Mario offered to help with the medical bills. After Roberto finished with radiation, the oncologist ran the tests again. The good news was that the tumor became very small and Roberto could resume his life, as soon as he felt back to himself.

Two months later, he was back at work with Ariana. Roberto would leave by 3:00 p.m. from the office and pick up Robbie, who was now one year old and so adorable. He was walking and so smart. Ariana and Roberto started to feel positive again; they read to Robbie, and he could make all the animal sounds and started called Roberto *Da* and Ariana *mama*. They were still so much in love. Roberto's hair started to grow back.

Reprieve

Ariana and Roberto resumed their normal life and went to their parents' house for Sunday dinners, and Vincenzo, Lorenzo, and Maria's parents made Sunday a special family time. Everyone held Robbie and kissed him. He was Ariana's grandparents' first great-grandson. Bella and Giovani had a baby girl and named her Rosemarie. Mario had not made his usual trips to Palermo, as they were all consumed with Roberto's sickness and supporting Ariana and watching the baby. Mario decided it was time to check on the business and see his second grandchild. Maria went with him to see her new granddaughter and see her son and Bella, whom she missed.

Roberto and Ariana had been taking Robbie to work with them and had a playpen, and his toys there. He was so good and entertained himself and very rarely cried. The clients that came loved seeing the beautiful baby. Everything seemed to be going well, and Maria's father took care of the tomatoes and canning for Mario while he was in Palermo.

Mario and Maria adored their granddaughter and were both tearful when they left to return home. Maria's parents were now seventy-eight and eighty. Maria noticed them slowing down, although her mother still cooked in the evening and for Sunday dinner, but she sat on a stool instead of standing. Her father seemed to urinate often and was up three to four times at night to urinate. Mario insisted that he see a urologist. It was found that he had an enlarged prostate, and he was set up for a biopsy, which was questionable. The urologist said, "An enlarged prostate at his age is normal." The doctor said he would see him again in three months.

One month later, he started urinating some blood. He did not tell anyone, but Francesca saw it in the toilet bowl when Antonio forgot to flush. They rushed him to the hospital, and scans were done. They were told he had an aggressive prostate cancer. Maria and her mother were furious with the urologist who missed the diagnosis and did not want to see him for three months. Mario said, "We should sue him." Antonio started having pain and was prescribed pain medication as the doctor in the hospital mentioned that with aggressive prostate, it may have spread. Antonio died in his sleep when he was eighty-one.

Francesca was inconsolable as they had been married fifty-nine years, and she felt that half of her was gone. They had a funeral mass, and Francesca wanted him cremated so she could keep him beside her on the table next to her bed. Maria and Mario felt the loss, and both felt depressed for all they went through this past year. Everyone missed him and felt the loss for a long time. Maria felt the loss of her father, who was always there for her and loved the grandchildren. She feared her mother getting older and the potential loss of her one day. The good part was having two beautiful and healthy grandchildren. Maria was especially worried that what they had been through was enough and went to church every day and prayed all the sorrow would end and everyone would continue to be healthy.

Maria was now fifty, and Mario was fifty-two. They both felt good and were very active.

Ariana and Roberto continued to make money in their accounting firm.

Vincenzo and Lorenzo were very successful architects and went out to club one night. They met two friends who were only at the club for a bachelorette party. Both girls were very pretty and stared at the handsome two brothers. They went for coffee with them and talked like they were old friends. Each of the brothers separately asked the girls on a date. Lorenzo took Gianna to an Italian restaurant, while Vincenzo took Cecilia to a French restaurant and then to a fair.

Both boys talked about their dates and decided they felt serious about the girls for the first time. They continued seeing them and had a couple of dates together. Gianna was a pediatric nurse practitioner in a private office, while Cecilia studied dance in college, was now a dance instructor, and had her own studio. They dated the girls for about six months. Vincenzo bought a large round 2k diamond ring and proposed to Cecilia Marino, and she said yes right away. Lorenzo proposed to Gianna Greco six months after Vincenzo bought a beautiful large pear-shaped diamond and asked her to marry him. Gianna said yes.

The boys finally found girls that they loved. Maria and Mario were thrilled that the boys met nice girls to marry. The boys were older when they fell in love because they devoted so much time to working at their firm. The four of them decided on a double wedding. The girls were friends and shopped together with their mothers for different wedding gowns. They had a large wedding with family and friends. Giovani and Bella came with their darling baby girl, and Maria's sisters and Mario's sister and brother came. Maria's mother became tearful at the church, as she remembered her own wedding to Francisco. The wedding was on June 24, 1989, and was magnificent, and everyone enjoyed themselves.

Maria and her mother were so happy to see Centina and Alessandro, who looked old, and Canelora and Claudio. Maria and Mario were happy his sister Chiara and her husband, Matteo, and his brother Carmen and his wife, Bianca, came also. They were so happy that everyone flew for the double wedding. Maria had not seen all her family together for a long time. They all felt the loss of their father and that he would have been proud of his grandsons having a double wedding. Maria and Mario's family continues to grow, and they are happy looking forward to more grandchildren and great-grandchildren for her mother and Mario's mother, who did not make it to the wedding due to arthritic pain.

Maria noticed her sisters got so much older-looking. The years were passing quickly. The boys went on separate honeymoons with their new wives. Vincenzo and Cecilia went to the Bahamas for a week, and Lorenzo and Gianna went on a week cruise to the

Caribbean. When they all returned, the boys resumed the architectural firm, and the girls continued to work.

At one of the Sunday dinners, Vincenzo and Cecilia announced they were expecting a baby and Cecilia was three months pregnant. Lorenzo and Gianna, five weeks later at another Sunday dinner, announced they were pregnant. Maria and Mario could not believe the wonderful news. Maria wished her father were still alive to hear how many great-grandchildren he would have.

New Happenings

Ariana and Roberto continued to work together at their accounting office and had a large client base, which kept growing as clients referred them to other people. Businesses always had accounting needs, and during tax season, they were extremely busing and worked long hours. Robbie sometimes fell asleep during their late days. All their clients loved to see Robbie and talked and played with him while waiting for them to finish their taxes.

Roberto had to go to the oncologist every six months for scans, just to make sure he was doing well. Roberto went to bed as soon as he showered after they got home from the office. He sometimes went to bed at 9:00 p.m. Ariana became concerned, as sometimes it was 8:00 p.m., and he fell asleep instantly. When Ariana questioned him, he said, "Working so many hours with the computer and adding machine leaves my eyes tired, and I look forward to a night's sleep."

Months went by since the double wedding, and Vincenzo and Cecilia announce at a Sunday dinner that they were expecting a baby in six months. Everyone was happy. Maria's mother still wore black as she still missed her husband every day, but the double wedding and the thought of another new great-grandchild made her happy that she lived long enough to have great-grandchildren. The new baby would make her third great-grandchild.

Maria assumed she would watch the new baby after Cecilia resumed her dance studio and her boys were busy in their architectural firm. Seven weeks later, Vincenzo and Gianna brought a positive pregnancy stick to another Sunday dinner, and Maria screamed with joy, but Mario did not understand why she screamed until she showed him the positive pregnancy stick. The family celebrated another grandchild. The family was growing, and Maria was glad they bought a big house and would have to buy a larger dining room table. She called Giovani and Bella to tell them the good news and was told by Giovani that Bella was expecting again and to have a child in 5 months. Maria and Mario were ecstatic about all the new grandchildren coming.

On November 8, 1989, Giovani and Bella called to tell them all Bella had a natural delivery at the hospital and had a 7.5-pound baby boy, named Luca. They sent pictures, and he was a beautiful baby. Rosemarie was now 2 ½, very smart, and kind to her little baby brother. She kissed him every morning. Maria planned to go to Palermo the next time Mario went to see her two grandchildren there.

Bella and Giovani spoke Italian at home. They both took English in high school, but since they and their friends spoke Italian, they did not get much of a chance to practice English. Mario and Maria went to Palermo two months after Luca was born. They spoke Italian when in Palermo. Luca was baptized while they were there, and Bella and Giovani asked Maria and Mario to be the godparents. They both felt so honored to be Luca's godparents. Maria cried when they left to come home, as she hated to leave those sweet grandchildren and her son and Bella. Giovani said, "When Luca and Rosemarie get a little older, we will come for a visit, maybe at Christmas."

When Maria and Mario came home, Cecilia looked like she would have the baby any minute. Three days later, she was in labor, and Vincenzo took her to the hospital, and he stayed through the delivery and took pictures of the birth. They all stayed in the lobby of the hospital, waiting to hear any news. Four hours later, Vincenzo came out to tell them they had a son. He was so excited and told them how well Cecilia did and she took no medication. They named him Matteo, who was born on March 10, 1990.

Maria realized how delivery had changed since she had her children. Now fathers were there for the birth. Three weeks later, Gianna went into labor, and Lorenzo brought her to the hospital and of course stayed with her throughout labor and delivery. He ran to the lobby to tell his parents they had a baby boy, and they named him Leonardo, who was born on March 28, 1990. Both boys were so happy that the cousins would be close in age and go to school together. All four of them again decided to have them christened together in two months and have a huge party after church at the Knights of Columbus with a band and catered Italian food. Lorenzo and Vincenzo felt bad that Giovani's son, who was also almost the same age as their sons, were not there. Giovani would never leave his business to move here, but maybe Bella and Luca would come and spend summers in America when they get older.

All three babies were beautiful, and Maria and Mario felt the same feeling when they raised their three sons before Ariana was born. Maria watched her grandsons whenever she was needed. Cecilia and Gianna were breastfeeding and took at least ten weeks off before they returned to work. Vincenzo and Cecilia stayed in the apartment that the brothers used to share. Lorenzo and Gianna bought a beautiful large house in Garden City. The brothers had a very successful and thriving architectural firm. Vincenzo and Cecilia were planning to look for a house also in Garden City.

All three of Maria and Mario's new grandsons were gaining weight and were very healthy. They still went to mass and prayed and were thankful for their growing family.

Roberto had his six-month scans, and the oncologist wanted to meet with him to discuss the results. Ariana was always on the edge and worrying. Ariana's grandmother said to her, "Ariana, tu ha una proprio nel cento della fronte." Ariana was always so beautiful, but the strain of worrying about Roberto caused her to have a wrinkle in the middle of her forehead, which was what her grandmother said.

Ariana looked in the mirror, and she also noted crow's feet by her eyes and also noticed wrinkles starting around her mouth. Ariana went with Roberto to the oncology office. Her hands were shaking when Dr. Gerstein told Roberto the tumor was back. Roberto made the decision he did not want to go through chemotherapy again. He would do radiation to buy more time. He was set up to start radiation in three days. When they returned from the doctor's office, they went to her parents' home to pick up Robbie. Her grandmother looked at

Ariana again and said, "Si. Siembri depresso. Cosa e successo?" Her grandmother said she looked depressed and asked what happened. Ariana burst into tears and could not speak. Her grandmother then said, "Ciao, Roberta, che si dice?" She asked Roberto what was up. Maria told her mother to stop asking questions as she was upsetting them both.

Ariana told her mother in private that the cancer was back and Roberto would only do radiation because he refused chemo again. Ariana tried to be strong for Roberto and Robbie. Maria and Mario were so happy, but in a second, all that had changed, and they worried for her daughter and Roberto. Ariana had suspected a problem when Roberto went to bed early and had to be woken up in the morning for work. He finally admitted to her after they saw the doctor that his headaches were back. He said when he went to bed and slept, his headaches were relieved. Roberto wanted to keep working, but Ariana told him no. He was to start radiation, and Mario again offered to take him. The doctor had also prescribed pain medication for his headaches. Ariana prayed every time that the radiation would shrink the tumor. Ariana would cry herself to sleep, wishing the tumor in his brain could be surgically removed. Roberto started to feel worse.

Sadness

The radiation on Roberto's head shrunk the tumor a bit. The oncologist just wanted to relieve his headaches and also gave him pain medication. The oncologist offered him another four weeks of radiation every day. Ariana begged Roberto to try the additional treatment. He said he would try but that it makes him so tired. He went through the additional four weeks of radiation, and he became so fatigued and had burns on the back if his head. Dr. Gerstein, the oncologist, did another scan and told them the tumor shrunk a bit more. He told them he had hoped it had shrunk more and that it is an aggressive cancer and the first time there was a longer time for it to grow again. He suggested, "If you still have headaches when you recover from the radiation, the next step is hospice."

Ariana started suffering with anxiety attacks and could not catch her breath. Roberto recovered from radiation and attempted to go back to work with Ariana, but he started to become dizzy and fainted at work. Ariana called for emergency assistance, and an ambulance brought him to the hospital. His blood tests were abnormal, and the cancer antigen was very high. Ariana wanted to bring him home to her mother's house and get hospice, but she needed her family's support and to spend time with Robbie.

Roberto became weaker and weaker and loved to hold his son. Ariana brought Robbie in to see his father. Ariana held Robbie when Roberto hugged him. Robbie was now two-and-a-half years old, and he became confused as to why his father stayed in bed and did not play with him. A nurse from hospice came twice a week and taught Ariana how to give him pain medication and anti-anxiety meds.

The sadness permeated the house. Ariana lay next to him at night. She still loved him and hated to see him suffer. Roberto tried to be positive for Ariana, but he was too weak to get up, and his headaches were barely touched with the strong pain medication. He started to run a fever, and breathing became difficult, as the tumor was at the center in the base of his brain, which controls many important life functions. When he became so weak and had difficulty breathing, Ariana knew the end was near, and although she loved him so much, she wished his suffering would end.

Roberto died on August 5, 1976. He was the love of Ariana, and they were only married four years and three months. Roberto being sick and dying was not part of the plan; they were supposed to get old together. Roberto's parents and brother came to see him when he became very ill, and they stayed for the funeral mass and burial. Ariana just went through the motions and spent the rest of the week sobbing like her heart would break. Robbie asked for his daddy and cried. They had to tell him Daddy loved him so much but he got so sick and went to heaven.

Roberto's parents and brother went home the day after the funeral. Ariana could not function for over two weeks. She went through all the stages of grief. She was sad, depressed, angry at things like why her grandmother who was now over eighty and Roberto died so young. She was angry it happened and started bargaining. She had so many thoughts, even thinking about having another baby with the saved sperm taken before he started chemo so she would have another part of him. She felt confused and missed Roberto so much. She started to talk to him when she was alone and wanted to go back to her apartment with her son. Maria worried about her daughter and stopped over almost every day to see how she was and check on Robbie. Ariana was well aware to stay positive with Robbie and only cried and talked to Roberto when he was sleeping. Even though he was gone, Ariana still felt his presence. She made the decision she would get impregnated with his sperm and have a sibling for

Robbie. She went to a reproductive health doctor to start the process. Ariana did not tell her mother what she planned, as she was afraid others would disapprove or try to discourage her.

Christmas

The Christmas holidays would be a time of new beginning. Thanksgiving was quiet; the family came to eat at their parents' home. Ariana was a bit late, and her mother worried, but she came with Robbie. The dinner was good, and as soon as a normal conversation began, Ariana made an excuse that she was going home to put Robbie to bed and left early, and her mother gave her some of the food to take home.

Right after Thanksgiving, Maria and Mario went out and bought a large real tree and decorated it. Maria also decorated the house. Giovani, Bella, and their two children were coming to stay with them the day before Christmas Eve and would stay a week later.

Ariana still met with the reproductive doctor who inseminated her with Roberto's sperm. It took right away, and she found out she was pregnant on November 4, 1976. She felt excited to tell the family when all her brothers and their families were there for Christmas. Maria's mother, who was now eighty-three, still helped with several trays of lasagna, meatballs, and a large antipasto, and she made her famous cannoli for dessert. Grandma Francesca loved her grandchildren and great-grandchildren.

Vincenzo and Lorenzo came to help their father put up all the outdoor Christmas lights. The whole house looked like a Christmas wonderland. Maria worried that Ariana would be depressed at not having Roberto for the festive holiday. The house was all ready for the family who were all coming for Christmas Eve and Christmas Day. Maria was busy shopping for her children and grandchildren. For her children, she bought expensive outfits. For the older grandchildren, she bought clothes, and for Robbie and Rosemarie, she bought iPods so that they could download music and the latest iPads. Their fathers and uncles helped set them up for them at Christmas. She bought appropriate toys for the little grandchildren and books. Mario and Maria wrapped all the Christmas presents and put them under the tree next to the manger with baby Jesus.

The time between Thanksgiving and Christmas went so fast, and they were looking forward to seeing Giovani, Bella, Rosemarie, and Luca. Giovani, Bella, and the kids arrived at Kennedy Airport at 2:30 p.m., and Mario picked them up. When they came in, Maria ran to greet them and kissed and hugged them all. Rosemarie was now almost three and beautiful and so talkative and smart. Luca was almost seven weeks and smiling at everyone and making adorable sounds. Lorenzo, Gianna, and Leonardo, who was nine months old, got there first. An hour later, Vincenzo, Cecilia, and 9-month-old Matteo came. Ariana and Robbie came shortly after. Robbie was fourteen and so handsome. Maria and Mario adored all the beautiful grandchildren. The three boys and Ariana were so happy to be together and kept talking to one another. Maria was glad Ariana looked happy. Maria's mother stopped wearing black and looked pretty in her rose dress and was so happy she knew her great-grandchildren.

After eating a large antipasto Maria and her mother made, they all went to church on Christmas Eve, at the 4:00 p.m. mass so that in the morning, the kids could open presents. It was a beautiful mass, and Christmas songs were sung. Maria felt so blessed that her whole family was at mass together. She thanked God for all she had.

When they all returned from church, Maria put out a lot of hors d'oeuvres, both hot and cold, for Christmas Eve. She cooked vegetables and cut up small pieces of chicken for the nine-month-old grandsons, and Bella fed Luca. They had a lovely evening, and the young kids went to bed early. The adults had glasses of wine and watched Christmas shows on TV. Maria thought it was strange that Ariana just wanted some soda, as she claimed she was so thirsty from the antipasto earlier. Ariana and Robbie went home, as she had put up a tree and bought Robbie presents that he would open early, and said they would be back at her parents' house by 10:00 am.

There were so many gifts under the tree, and Maria and Mario handed the parents the gifts for them and their young children. Rosemarie opened her own gifts. Robbie was overwhelmed at more gifts, and Ariana loved her gifts. The kids even bought their parents gifts. Maria was so pleased that everyone loved their gifts. After all the wrapping was cleaned up and everyone showed each other their gifts, Maria made a big breakfast for everyone. By the time breakfast was cleaned up, it was almost 1:00 p.m. The lasagna trays were very thick, and they wanted to eat Christmas dinner about 3:00 p.m. Maria put them in the oven as they would take a while to cook. Maria would heat the meatballs later and make small noodles for the babies and cut up a meatball for them.

Leonardo and Matteo spent their time in the playpen together playing with toys. They were used to being together and only had a couple of weeks' difference in age, and they were adorable together. They ate dinner at 3:15 p.m., and Maria made a tremendous number of meatballs and extra sauce. There was also sausage in the lasagna. Everyone raved about the dinner. Leonardo and Matteo loved their small pasta with a little sauce and cut-up meatballs, true little Italian boys.

Ariana announced over dinner she had something to tell everyone. She told them she was six weeks pregnant with Roberto's baby. Maria and Mario and the entire family were shocked. She tried to explain she was very happy to be pregnant with Roberto's saved sperm before he had chemo. If he were still living, he would have been glad for a second child. She said, "I feel closer to him carrying his baby. Robbie will have a sibling, and he thought it was exciting." Since Robbie has been in school, his name was Roberto Jr. When everyone absorbed it, they congratulated her, and Maria realized why she did not have any wine. Maria and Mario were happy about a new grandbaby. Her brothers thought it was great, and the boys and their wives kissed and hugged her. She was still working at the accounting firm and had made a lot of money and decided to buy a house in Massapequa to be close to her parents.

Lorenzo and Vincenzo both had beautiful homes in Garden City. It was a wonderful and memorable 1990 Christmas. Giovani and Bella stayed until New Year's Day. During the week, they went into the city and saw the play *Wicked*. Robbie and Maria's mother came too. A good friend of Maria's came to the house to watch the little ones while they went to Manhattan. They went to see the tree at Rockefeller Plaza also and St. Patrick's Cathedral to pray and lit candles. They all went to Mamma Leone's for a delicious dinner. They took the train, and on the way home, everyone was tired, especially Maria's mother. Mario held her arm wherever we walked. She fell asleep on the train and was awakened when they were near their stop.

Maria told the children that on January 6th was the epiphany and Befana, the good witch, brings the children gifts in that day. Maria bought small gifts for the children and told them Befana brought them. They parked the car, so they drove everyone back to the house. Maria made her usual Sunday dinner on New Year's Eve. Ariana, Vincenzo and Cecilia, and Lorenzo and Gianna all said their goodbyes to Giovanni and Bella and kissed their beautiful children. They missed them. All the others went home after dinner and welcomed 1991 in their own homes.

Maria and Mario were so sad to say goodbye to them in the morning before Mario drove them to the airport. It was a wonderful week with their family. On September 20, 1991, Ariana was in labor, and her mother stayed with her while she was in labor and for the birth of a beautiful baby girl. The labor was easy this time, and she delivered in four hours. Maria was so happy having her second granddaughter. Ariana named her Roberta. Ariana's son, Roberto Jr., was happy to be having a baby sister to love and protect. Ariana found a lovely house in North of Merrick Rd. in Massapequa, which was close to her parents. She decorated the home beautifully yet cozy. Roberto Jr. loved the house and stayed in the same school, as he made a lot of friends. Maria watched the baby when Ariana went back to work.

July 1992

Maria's mother, Francesca, was becoming very frail and started to be a bit confused. She asked when her husband would be home. Maria was concerned as her mother always had energy and helped her with everything and she loved her great-grandchildren. She did not have her normal appetite. It was like she just gave up. She was now eighty-seven, and Maria thought she would live past ninety, but she had a good life and saw many great-grandchildren. She stayed in bed now most of the time, as she was too weak to get up. Maria took great care of her. Maria called the priest to come to the house for last rites. He came, and they all said prayers with the priest over her mother. She died at 4:00 p.m., July 15, 1992.

Maria cried her like her heart would break. Her mother was strong, and Maria counted on her for help. They had a funeral mass, and the priest knew her well and said wonderful thigs about her mother. Mario got up and said what a wonderful person she was and that he will miss her every day. Maria could not speak, as she was overcome with emotion. She remembered when they lived in Palermo raising her children and her parents lived close and walked over almost every day. Now Maria has lost both of her wonderful parents. She grieved for a long time. Maria felt she could not look at her parents' room in her house, as it was so painful. She had it repainted and beds discarded and bought a sauna and put in in the room. She felt as Mario and her were getting older, the sauna would help them.

Mario still made his trips to check on the business in Palermo. Mario and Maria were married forty-five years. Maria was now fifty-four and Mario fifty-six. Mario stayed longer in Palermo, and when he went to a supermarket to buy some food, he met a beautiful woman in her forties. He spoke Italian to her, and they both started talking. Her name was Rosa, and she invited him to her home for coffee. He agreed, and he was so attracted to her and she to him. He did give it any thought, and they made passionate love. He saw her five more times when he was there and made love each time. He told his son when he was in Palermo that he liked to take long walks. He told Rosa when he comes back in a couple of months, he would see her and call her if he could. They kissed, and he left for home the next day.

When he got home from Palermo and kissed Maria, he felt guilty. They were married for forty-five years, and Mario felt she was more interested in the grandchildren than him. They made love rarely now.

Maria had gone to the store, and Mario found it a good time to call Rosa. Maria only needed a few items for dinner at the store. When she got home from the store, she heard Mario on the phone and heard him say, "Rosa, I enjoyed our time together and miss you and cannot wait to be together again."

Maria could not believe what she heard. Maria never yelled or cursed. She said, "Who the fuck do you think you are? We are married for forty-five years. My parents were married fifty-nine years and were together always. Your trips to Palermo were to check on your business, not to meet someone. You can leave and go to her, and you will continue to pay the bills in this house. Get out, you cheating old goat. If she is young, she will tire of you, but don't come back to me. When the boys hear what you did, they will not want to see you."

Mario walked out and did not know where to go or what to do. He could not keep the tomato canning business, and he knew apologizing would not help, as Maria was too angry. Maria decided to get help from her sons to take over the tomato canning business herself. Vincenzo and Lorenzo helped Maria start the business and also the imports and arrange the trucks for transporting. Maria would keep busy running the business herself. Maria started to wonder about other indiscretions he may have committed. Maria felt she could never trust him again. When she was alone, she cried about losing her mother and then her marriage, which she thought would last till death do them part. Mario promised this in the Catholic church. He was the one who broke the vows. She would prove she was capable of making money.

Maria also called Giovani and filled him on his father's activity when he was last in Palermo. Giovani was disgusted and remembered when he caught his father with the female worker with her blouse off and his father fondling her breast. He told Giovani, who was young at the time, he was so sorry and please not to tell his mother. Giovani never told his mother until this terrible news and proceeded to tell her what he found when his father ran the company. Giovani said, "That is why I fired her as soon as I took over." Maria was again shocked that this happened a long time ago, and it just reinforced her decision not to forgive Mario. Giovani said, "He will not stay in this house if he comes back. He can find a hotel room."

Maria saw her doctor and told him the stress she was under, losing her mother and then her forty-five-year marriage. The doctor prescribed a low-dose antidepressant and a tranquilizer, only when she needed it and to help her sleep. Although Maria did feel sad, she finally felt in control and looked forward to running the part of the business, while Giovani continued to run the business in Palermo. Maria would also watch Roberta while Ariana worked. Ariana also told her mother she would help her in the business on evenings and on the weekend. Mario tried calling Maria, but she refused to answer any calls from him.

Going It Alone

Maria enjoyed her new life, and the antidepressant medication helped her focus on the business. She finally had a sense of purpose other than being a housewife. She still cooked Sunday dinners for her children and grandchildren but was busy the rest of the week. Listening to Mario always talking about his successes led her to believe it was only a man's job. She proved him wrong, and she became just as successful as he was. Her sons and daughter were so proud of her. She visited Giovani every three months to see how he was doing with production and of course to see her two beautiful grandchildren, who were growing up so fast. Rosemarie was in second grade, while Leonardo was five and in kindergarten. They grew so fast, it seemed her grandchildren grew faster than her own children. Maria felt as she got older, the years flew by.

Giovani was handling the business in Palermo great and sending the wines and olive oil, and Maria had the trucks pick them up from the docks and distribute to the markets and liquor stores. Maria was proud of herself running the business and also the growing tomatoes and the canning process and distribution with the trucks. Mario had made enough of his own money in the past and had enough to live on living alone. Maria did not care if he was in Palermo with his young girlfriend or elsewhere. She had no contact with him, and Maria was sure when he finds out she was running the business, he would realize he can be replaced. She felt she was busy all the time. She still made Sunday dinners, and her two sons and Ariana came.

The years went fast, and it was 1996, and Maria and Mario had not spoken for four years. Roberta was now in full-time kindergarten, and Ariana continued the successful accounting firm she and Roberto had started. She was doing well and had two employees helping her. She would pick Roberta at her bus stop and bring her to the office. She was a very good little girl and sat and drew pictures until Ariana was done for the day. She would bring her home and make dinner for her and Roberto Jr., who was now twenty-three. He was very handsome and had many girls interested in him. He had gone to college to be an accountant like his mother and father. He passed the CPA exam and started to work with his mother. One of Ariana's employees wanted to retire, and Roberto Jr. took the spot and did very well. He was very smart and made money for the firm and was reimbursed handsomely.

Roberto Jr. loved his little sister. Roberto Jr. used to go to the gym after work and dinner, and he met Mia Farina there. He had noticed that she came to the gym several times a week. Roberto Jr. started to talk to her, and soon they began dating. He brought her home to meet his mother and little sister. Ariana loved her for her son. They dated for a year, and she came to his grandmother's Sunday dinners. Everyone liked her.

He proposed to her, and they were married six months later. Roberto Jr. was twenty-six, and Mia was twenty-four. Mia was an executive in an advertising firm. Her parents paid for a beautiful reception after getting married in the church. The wedding was on June 17, 1999. Mia's sister, Mariana, was her maid of honor and had three friends in the wedding party. Roberto Jr. had a good friend as his best man and two friends in his wedding party, and his little sister was a junior bridesmaid. It was a great wedding, and everyone had fun. Ariana felt bad that her father could not see his first grandson's wedding. She knew her mother, who was there for the family, would not want him there. Mia and Roberto Jr. went on a ten-day trip to Italy, and when they returned, both went back to work. They moved into a brand-new beautiful apartment and bought new furniture and had so many household items from Mia's wedding shower. They both had good jobs and could afford the rent on the beautiful apartment with a huge balcony.

Taking Him In

Maria got a phone call at 3:00 a.m. She jumped up and immediately thought something happened to her kids or grandchildren. Her heart was hammering when the person stated he was Dr. Haan from Mt. Sinai South Nassau Hospital. He explained he has been seeing Mario and he has aggressive metastatic cancer. The doctor said he was treated with chemo, but the next scan showed more sites. He advised he be put on hospice, as he does not have long to live. The doctor explained he looked in his wallet and found that she was his wife. The doctor apologized for waking her at this hour but said Mario took a turn for the worse. "He had stated he did not want us to call you, but I felt I had no choice as he was alone in an apartment in Freeport."

Maria stated she would be there in the morning. In the morning, she called Vincenzo and Lorenzo and explained the situation. The boys took her to the hospital, and Mario looked so old and sick. His skin and eyes were yellow. The doctor came in to talk to them and said, "The cancer was metastatic and spread to his liver and lung. There is nothing more that can be done. You can take him home and get hospice that will keep him comfortable with medication, or he can go to the hospice facility. It is up to you and your family, as I know you have been estranged for four years."

When they left the hospital, Maria talked it over with her sons. She also spoke to Ariana who was already at work. Maria's sons and daughter felt since Mario was dying, he should come home where he would be cared for. Maria made sure hospice would come to bathe him and provide medication for pain. Maria had a hospital bed put downstairs. She felt it was strange having him back in the house after 4 years had passed. She was relieved to find that he had not been in Palermo with the past girlfriend and found he had an apartment in Freeport by the water.

She checked on him and asked him if he needed anything. He answered, "It is hard for me to eat anything and can only sip water that is not cold."

Maria felt he looked so much older and weak. He had difficulty and even used energy to talk. He had difficulty breathing. She asked him if he was in pain, and all he did was nod his head, indicating he was in pain.

The hospice nurse had given them liquid morphine with a dropper. She gave him the dose indicated. Hospice sent an aide to wash him and brush his teeth. He could not get to the bathroom as he was bedridden. The aide tried to hold the urinal from him, but the urine wound up in the bed. The next step was pads on the bed, which had to be changed frequently. Lorenzo or Vincenzo would change the pads. Maria had to keep the business running and left hospice or the boys to care for their father. At night, she had to do it, but he slept most of the time.

Ariana came with the two children, and Mario perked up when he saw her and her daughter, whom he had never met. Roberto Jr. and his wife came for a short visit. Mario was exhausted after the visits. Maria checked on him a few times during the night, and he was no longer alert. He began muttering and said, "That witch or bitch left me and stole my business." Then he proceeded to mumble but no words. He cried out like he was in pain, and Maria gave him his dose of pain medication and pulled his throat so he would swallow it.

Maria checked on him in the morning, and his breathing was slow and moist with noises. She sat with him and held his hand, and he took a shuddering breath, which was his last one. She called the hospice, and they sent the nurse to pronounce him dead. Her sons and daughter made arrangements for a funeral mass and then cremation. They sent the ashes to Giovani in Palermo to sprinkle the ashes in the Mediterranean sea, which Mario loved and was close to home where life was good.

Giovani and Bella and the children could not come for the mass and felt bad that they had not seen Mario for four years but did not want to see him sick and dying. Giovani felt, by putting his ashes where they were all a happy family, he was doing his part to put his father to rest. After Maria witnessed Mario's death, she cried herself to sleep remembering all the good years they spent together and reminisced about their love and wedding. She decided she would not dwell on the hurt she experienced with Mario's behavior but remember all the great years they had and how he loved their children and grandchildren. Mario died at 60 years old on March 2, 1988.

Life Goes On

Maria was fifty-eight years old and still running the successful business. She felt well and realized that her sons and her daughter were successful in their chosen fields and had no desire to run the business. Maria continued to run the business until she felt it was time to stop. She had made lot of money and invested a in a large 401 K. She invested wisely and could live on proceeds from her 401(k) for her entire life. Her children's ages were getting older—Ariana was thirty-six, Lorenzo thirty-seven, Vincenzo thirty-eight, and Giovani thirty-nine.

Lorenzo and Vincenzo both decided they wanted another child before they were forty. Lorenzo and Gianna got pregnant first. She was due on January 4, 1989. Vincenzo and Cecilia took a bit later to get pregnant. Cecilia was due April 28. Everyone was happy, especially that their second children again would be close in age. Maria was so happy, as she would now have eight grandchildren and one great-grandchild. Roberto Jr. had a son and named him Carlo. Ariana made a wonderful grandmother and loved Carlo with her whole heart. Maria realized that none of her children would have four children like she did. She had been a stay-at-home mother, but today, women worked outside of their home and made great money, allowing them to go on vacation when they want.

Maria offered to watch the new babies until they were old enough to go into child care. Maria felt she was stretched thin with the business and watching two infants. The babies' names were Aldo and Riccardo. Maria's great-grandson's name was Alessio. Her sons and daughters-in-law realized it was a lot for Maria, and Cecilia and Gianna decided to get a babysitter, who would watch the boys together. The woman was an old family friend, and both houses in Garden City had security cameras inside the house and all around the house. Both babies would be watched at Vincenzo and Cecilia's house. Cecilia had more flexibility and stopped home just to check on everything. The babysitter, Mia, handled both babies well and sang to them.

Maria resumed her hectic schedule and went over to check on her grandsons and just held them and kissed them. Maria was always busy and took a trip to Palermo to check in with Giovani and how he was doing and of course to visit with her grandchildren there. Maria adored all of her eight grandchildren and her great-grandson. She felt she had a wonderful life now and still had the Sunday dinners. Maria wished Giovani, Bella, and the children could also be part of the Sunday family time, but he had to grow the grapes for the wine and the olives for the olive oil.

Maria took over growing the tomatoes and canning them. The trucks kept everything going smoothly, picking up the imports at the docks and distributing and also picking up the canned Italian tomatoes and distributing them. The truck drivers liked working for Maria and on their own added some new contacts to bring the products to.

The years started to fly by as Maria got older trying to keep the businesses going. She was getting tired of keeping the big house too. Before she knew it, she was sixty-eight, and although healthy, she did not want to run the businesses any longer. She spoke to her older son, Giovani, and asked if he had a strong worker who was younger and could run the business in Palermo. She also wanted to rent the house in Palermo and have his family consider moving to America and buying the house in Massapequa to take over the tomato business. She told him, "It is a year-round business, with the hot house, which your father had built." The money from the Palermo wine and olive oil business would still bring money for Giovani while paying his great friend who knew the entire business a huge salary, which was enough to pay for renting the house in Palermo. He would continue growing the grapes and olives and sending the wine and olive oil to the docks in New York. The trucks would still pick up at the docks and deliver them to the stores and Italian markets.

Giovani, Bella, Rosemarie, and Luca were excited to come to America to live there. Giovani was old and had been running the Palermo businesses since he was young. He was excited for the change. The children were grown now. He had things to finish before he came, and the years continued to pass. It was 2005 when they came to America. Giovani was fifty-nine, Rosemarie was thirty-two and Luca was thirty. They both had graduated college, and Luca became an architect like his cousin, while Rosemarie studied accounting like her cousin, Ariana. She also passed her CPA. Both of them hoped to join their cousins' firms.

Time passed, and in 2005, Maria was seventy-seven, still very active and healthy. She had accrued a lot of money from running the businesses and her large 401(k) account. She was a wise business woman. She had researched a large condo on the ocean in West Long Beach, which she loved and cost $2,500,000. It was on the East Boardwalk and had three bedrooms and three and a half bathrooms, a large dining room, and kitchen. She would still have the family for Sunday dinners and had the time to cook. There was a balcony facing the ocean, and from most of the windows, she could see the ocean. She felt calm and happy and met some lovely neighbors. She was on the ninth floor. She loved decorating it and purchased all-new furniture and a large dining room set to accommodate the whole family. All the bedrooms were available if in the summer they may want to stay over to enjoy the beach. All of Maria's grandchildren were now grown. Roberto Jr. and his wife were expecting, and Maria would start a new chapter as a great-grandmother. Rosemarie joined Ariana's accounting firm and Ariana was thrilled to have help withe her cousin. Luca joined Vincenzo and Lorenzo's architectural firm and was happy that their cousin would be part of the firm, which would allow them more time off. Maria was ecstatic having her entire family together for Sunday dinners in her beautiful new condo. She had bought wonderful pieces of art to match the bedrooms and for the living room, and Maria was proud of her decorating skills.

New Happenings for Maria and Ariana

Maria was still a beautiful woman. She had always used olive oil on her skin in the mornings and evenings which caused her flawless, younger-looking skin. She maintained her lovely figure by exercise. She had learned to drive when they moved to Massapequa, and recently she purchased a sporty maroon BMW and had parking spot in the condo garage.

She was coming down the elevator to go to the Italian market to buy food for Sunday dinner when a handsome man got in the elevator first floor beneath her floor and said hello to her. She said hello to him back. They were both heading to the garage for their cars, and he introduced himself as John Gillen. She introduced herself. He was named after his father, but his mother was Italian, and her maiden name was Jordana Campinello. John said he grew up on Italian food. He asked if she was married, and she told him she was a widow. He shared with her that his wife died five years ago.

John asked Maria out for dinner the following Saturday evening. She said yes. He was very distinguished and told her that he was a lawyer. Maria felt good that she could still attract a man. She went to the store and bought all she needed for Sunday dinner.

It was Friday, and she mixed her meatballs and on Saturday made her sauce with meatballs and braciole. She would wait to make the pasta when the family comes Sunday. She set the table on

Saturday. The family all came, and the condo was full. She made an antipasto and got a few bottles of expensive red wine. While everyone was drinking wine and eating antipasto, Maria heated the sauce and made the pasta and cut up two loaves of seeded Italian bread.

The family was all talking and sharing the week's happenings. Ariana shared that she met someone who came in to seek accounting help. She said, "He was very handsome, and his name was Marco Savino, and he is an owner of a large investment firm." She stated, "I have seen him for 3 months and wanted to be sure it was serious before I tell everyone." The family was so happy for her, and everyone toasted for her.

Maria decided to "tell them she met a gentleman too and was going out to dinner with him next Saturday evening." The family was happy and toasted their mother too. When she told them his name, they were shocked, as it was not an Italian name, but Maria told them his mother was Italian and he grew up eating Italian food.

The weeks went by, and Ariana told everyone at a Sunday dinner at Maria's condo that she was getting married to Marco Savio, and she showed her beautiful engagement ring to the family. Marco came with her that Sunday she announced that they were getting married, as Ariana wanted her family to meet him. Maria opened a bottle of champagne to toast them. Everyone was very happy for Ariana, and they liked Marco right away. They were planning to get married in three months. Marco had two grown sons and two grandchildren. Marco had a beautiful large home in Brookville on the North Shore. Ariana sold her house for a good price, and she moved in with him. She still maintained her accounting firm and kept driving there from Brookville. Both Ariana and Marco planned their wedding and got married in the church. Ariana wore a lovely short white dress that was handmade by a dressmaker for her, and Marco wore a tuxedo. They had two good friends as best man and bridesmaid. They planned a wonderful reception in an Italian hall. The family came. Cousins of Ariana came, and Marco's parents, Salvatore and Silvana Savino, came. Marco's children and grandchildren and Ariana's children and grandchildren came. Everyone had a good time, and Maria and John danced great together.

Ariana and Marco went on a honeymoon to Tuscany for a week and then traveled south to Bari, where Marco's grandparents came from. When Marco and Ariana came back from their trip, they both went back to work.

Maria and John had only been sexually active with their dead spouses. When Maria and John had intercourse for the first time, they were both amazed at how sexually compatible they were. Maria used a lubricant but found the next time she did not need it, as Maria and John enjoyed each other and were both surprised to find how sexual they both were. They decided to keep both of their condos and spend time with each other in either condo, and when the family came for Sunday dinner, John was included. They did not include intimate details of their relationship, but they kissed each other when the children were around. When John's children and grandchildren visited him, Maria was also included. All their children were grown and may be able to deduce their relationship, but they did not want to actually tell them. They both felt the children may feel they were too old to have a sexual relationship.

C H A P T E R   1 9

Maria's Sisters

Maria used to call her sisters who were still both in Italy. She would call them on every holiday just to say hello. Maria knew she was getting old, although she felt good when she called Centina. She was told she was sick and told she was dying of heart failure. Maria was the youngest of the three sisters. She called Canelora and asked her why she was not told about Centina's condition. She answered, "Why? Could you have prevented it? I am getting old too, and I have had a broken hip repaired after falling. I get dizzy a lot. You have your life in America and your family there. We are both widows here in Italy, and our children are too busy with their families than to bother us."

When Maria hung up the phone, she realized how bitter Canelora was. Maria and John flew to Italy to see Centina before she died. They stayed two weeks, and she hugged her and told her she loved her. She was severely out of breath and smiled. She had a hospice nurse with her. A week later, she died. Her children arranged a funeral mass and burial. They were there for it.

Canelora came with a walker and looked so old and fragile, but she wanted to be at the mass and burial of her sister. Maria introduced John, and she said nothing, just stared. When Maria asked how she was doing, she said, "How do you think? I can't keep up my home, and I am going to an assisted living place, as my children and grandchildren do not want me living with them. With my husband's pension and selling my house, I can afford to stay here. After raising

60

my children, they are too busy to visit but found a place to put me. I guess I'll die here."

She hugged her and told her she would call her cell to see how she was making out. She couldn't wait to get on the plane with John and go home. Canelora was still miserable, and Maria could understand why her children did not want her to live with them. The next time she called to see how she was, she said she fell three times and banged her head and broke an arm. She asked her, "Why did you not press the button for help?"

She stated, "Who wants to help an old lady?"

Maria told her, "That is why you are there to get help before you fall." Maria called her children and told them to check on her and make sure she presses the button when she is dizzy before she falls and breaks more bones. Maria also told them to make sure she is eating.

She and John were still very happy and very close to both families. Maria was now seventy-eight, and John was three-and-a-half years younger than Maria. John will be seventy-five his next birthday. Maria found from Canelora's daughter that her sister's arm never healed from the break and the bang on her head left her with forgetfulness, and she had asked what happened to her arm. Canelora's children decided she needed to go to a nursing home, as she cannot maintain an apartment in assisted living. Maria felt very bad that one of her children would not care for her. Maria had both of her parents live with her. She knew her children would care for her if and when the time came. Maria believed that Canelora would wither away and die soon. Since she lost her husband and her children did not want to deal with her bitterness and depression, they rarely saw her. Maria felt that Canelora being in a nursing home would hasten her death. Six months after Canelora was put in the nursing home, she died in her sleep. Maria cried for her sisters and remembered them when they were young and when they came to America with their husband to weddings and to visit. When Mario and Maria lived in Palermo, her sisters and their families would come for the holidays. Maria worried that she was the last sister left. She stayed active, and John's love made her feel even younger than her years.

Concern and the Love That Prevailed

Everything seemed to be going along great with Maria and her children and grandchildren. One evening on March, Maria got a call from Bella, who told her Giovani was in the hospital because he had chest pain. Maria was very nervous, so John drove her to the hospital. Bella told Maria that Giovani was in cardiac catheterization lab. The cardiologist came out to talk to them and said, "Giovani did well and only a smaller cardiac vessel caused the pain, and a stent was place, and he will live a long life if he changes his diet and starts to exercise to lose some weight. I spoke with him about altering his diet to food like fish and vegetables or chicken. He must avoid heavy sauces and red meat. He can have some pasta with garlic and olive oil."

Everyone felt relieved, and the doctor sounded extremely positive. Giovani was picked up the next morning and went home. Maria came to the house to hug and kiss him and said Sunday dinners will reflect healthy for all. Maria will make delicious fish or chicken and pasta with garlic and olive oil. Giovani joined a gym, two weeks after he was hospitalized and the cardiologist gave him the approval. He lost a lot of weight and felt great. He kept the tomato business and caused no stress. Giovani believed the many years of stress running the business since he was young may have caused the medical issue. Everyone was so thankful that now everyone was healthy, as Maria had her other three children go for medical exams. Giovani was allowed red wine, and they toasted at Sunday dinner of delicious fish and many fresh vegetables.

Life was good, and the love from Maria for her family could be felt from her children, grandchildren, and great-grandchildren. She got married young, so even still in her seventies, she was already a great-grandmother. Maria and her children still went to mass each Sunday, and Maria lit candles at church and prayed to the Virgin Mary and God for blessing her with a wonderful family and the immense love that binds them all. Although life had ups and downs, it was a wonderful life for this Italian family who began in Palermo, Sicily, and made a beautiful transition to America while still maintaining their Italian heritage and devotion to the Catholic church. Sometimes, at Sunday dinners, they would spend a little time speaking Italian, as they did not want to forget their original language. Maria loved John, but her children and grandchildren always came first.

ABOUT THE AUTHOR

Carol Caico lives in a small town on Long Island. She has two wonderful sons and daughter-in-law's. She has four beautiful grandchildren, whom she adores. Her publications include several nursing and medical journal articles and a book, *Pathophysiology of Nursing Demystified*. She has a PhD and is a NP. This is her first novel. She enjoyed the process tremendously and even plans to continue writing novels.